"My Name Is Amelia"

DONALD J. SOBOL

A Joan Karl Book

ATHENEUM • 1994 • NEW YORK

Maxwell Macmillan Canada

Toronto

Maxwell Macmillan International

New York Oxford Singapore Sydney

Atheneum
Macmillan Publishing Company
866 Third Avenue
New York, NY 10022

Maxwell Macmillan Canada, Inc.
1200 Eglinton Avenue East
Suite 200
Don Mills, Ontario M3C 3N1

Macmillan Publishing Company is part of
the Maxwell Communication Group of Companies.

First edition
Printed in the United States of America
10 9 8 7 6 5 4 3 2 1
The text of this book is set in Aldine 401.

Library of Congress Card Catalog Number: 94-71878
ISBN 0-689-31970-3

In Memory of the Golden Boy

Robert Reinert

JANUARY 17, 1960—SEPTEMBER 14, 1989

Contents

Chapter 1

Girl Overboard

Shortly before midnight, sixteen-year-old Lisa Maddock tumbled overboard.

During the horror of falling, she reached wildly for a lifeline, brushed it with her fingertips, and plunged headlong. An instant later the dark Atlantic flooded over her.

She kicked desperately and came up twisting and gagging and spitting salt water. Off to her left she saw the light atop the mast of *Childhood II*.

She swam fewer than a dozen strokes. It was useless. The sloop was moving under power with the brainless obedience of fiberglass and steel. There was no chance of catching up.

Staying afloat was not an immediate problem. August had warmed the water to bathing temperature. Without a breeze to scuff the surface, the Atlantic lay as flat as marble, resting.

Don't lose your head, she thought, and put down panic by force of will. Another boat might be in the area.

She shouted at the top of her lungs. The night answered with black silence.

She recalled the crash. Just before she'd fallen overboard, *Childhood II* had hit something. The impact had thrown off a sickening crunch and clatter. The thirty-two-foot sloop had bucked violently, knocking her off her feet and into the ocean.

Whatever *Childhood II* had hit was still out there.

She worked around until she spotted a dark form riding low in the water.

She approached fearfully, using underwater strokes to avoid splashing. She could not be sure of it yet. It might be a plank. It might be a man-eater stunned by the collision.

She paused, pedaling in place, straining her eyes. It remained motionless, ignoring her.

She splashed. It did not move.

She swam again, quivering inside. Fifty yards more brought her within reach.

She stretched out an arm and touched a miracle—a log raft.

"Well, how do!" she gasped, not quite believing what sight and touch told her was there.

She groped for a hold, slipped, and dragged herself aboard on the second try. She rolled on her back, sprawling, limbs all apart, and let herself go. She thumped her fists and turned her head from side to side, hee-heeing in utter bliss as she watched her arms bounce off hard, solid wood.

When she had her fill of celebrating hope, she stood and stared after *Childhood II.*

The muffled beat of the thirty-horse diesel engine had faded out. When the wind had died at sunset, her sixth day at sea, she had dropped sail and gone to motoring. The unmanned sloop was following blindly the course she had set, throttle opened to five knots and rudder fixed.

Her last reckoning had put her east of the Caicos Islands in the Bahama chain. *Childhood II* was sure to be sighted, perhaps by a fishing boat or pleasure craft. Perhaps by a cruise ship. Lordy, lordy, the stir she'd create!

Lisa imagined the excitement, the questions—the headline:

IS GHOST SLOOP VICTIM
OF BERMUDA TRIANGLE?

The boarding party would see the wood panel with the Coast Guard registration. They'd find her documents and personal papers. Among the latter was a recent clipping from her hometown newspaper, the *Miami Times-Journal.* It described her as "Florida's water whiz."

I'll be waving at search planes before I'm thirsty, she told herself with more feeling than faith.

3

Childhood II receded steadily. Her masthead navigation light became a tiny white blob before being erased by the night. Lisa was alone in the empty sea.

Absolutely nothing could happen for a day or more.

The likelihood of being picked up by a passing ship before dawn was slim. She was sunk in darkness, without a flare to signal her presence. Nevertheless, she watched for an hour with stubborn patience.

Lisa Maddock had been in nasty spots before. She had always pulled through—usually by her wits, but if obliged, by her bodily courage.

The sea had bestowed a physical toughness rare in a teenager. Her arms, though lacking bulk, were firm and shapely. Her hips and legs seemed carved for scampering up a mast or trotting a deck in angry weather. Her hands and wrists, which people eventually noticed, were large and powerful.

Like so many active girls, she had grown impatient with the standard measurements of female conduct. Soccer, basketball, and softball had served as outlets for her energy until a red-faced boyfriend helped her discover a natural talent, arm wrestling.

She had never ducked a challenge, not even from Roxie, the waitress in Key West. A six-foot heavyweight with biceps as thick as a python, Roxie was a local attraction.

They had squared off on a stormy morning when the diner was crowded with weather-bound fishermen. For a good while their arms had stood like the hands of a clock stuck on noon. The diner was hot and their faces shone with sweat.

Lisa had offered a draw.

The fishermen had roared approval. Roxie, cheeks pumping, had growled, "Okay." Later, standing by the coffee urn behind the counter, she had sneaked Lisa a swift, meek look of thanks.

Adrift in the Atlantic, Lisa's strength had to be spent as wisely as in Key West. An ocean asks neither quarter nor gallantry. It simply waits.

"I'll beat you!" Lisa cried, and clenched her teeth against despair.

She knew the odds against her—at best, a hundred to one. She was trapped on a raft without sail, rudder, compass, food, or water.

Belief in herself was everything now.

She took off her deck shoes and propped them upside down to drain. She wrung out her shirt and shorts and bunched them into a respectable pillow.

Then she lay down under the stars.

She could do nothing but let the raft drift wherever it was bound.

Chapter 2

Adrift

Lisa rose to her feet as the horizon began to glow with the dawn. She had made it through the night.

Gradually the stars dimmed and the world lit. In all directions spread a blankness of water sealed to sky, an endless scene unmarked by time.

For a few seconds she forgot that she might nevermore see a tree, hear a bird sing, or be kissed. She felt as she always felt when watching the huge orange ball come up over the open sea: she had a front-row seat at a marvel, a glimpse of eternity.

Daybreak brought no sign of land. But the light gave her something, a good look at the raft.

It was an extraordinary piece of work. Lisa counted seven hand-sawed logs, about nine feet in length. The ends were held together by notched cross-logs and old-fashioned wooden pegs. Stout vines bound the middle.

Into both outside logs and the center log the builder had carved a grip. Lisa ran her hand along the bottom of the outside logs and felt a similar grip in both. If the raft flipped over, she could hang on.

Who had built the raft, and *why*? What danger could drive anyone to set off on such a craft in this day and age?

"Whoever you are and whatever your reason, I hope you made it home," Lisa murmured.

By eight o'clock the cloudless sky was shining bright. The sun blazed down with tropical warmth. It was going to be a hot one.

She put on her shorts and shirt and shoes and longed for better covering. From a damp hip pocket she drew a bandanna and tied it around her head, pirate style.

Besides the bandanna, she had a Swiss Army knife designed to do anything, and a waterproof wristwatch that was as advertised. It ran. She was in shape to face the day.

The raft rocked gently. A timid wind had risen. Here and there small whitecaps tumbled, glinting like pearls scattering.

As the morning wore on, Lisa found herself studying the western horizon for lengthy periods. In her mind she plotted her course.

If she was right—if she had fallen overboard east of the Caicos Islands, some 180 miles north of Haiti—she might reach the islands in one to three days. The ocean current ran in that direction, westward.

She put her progress at about one knot—this was only a guess. No fixed points existed by which to judge the rate of drift. The raft might be bobbing in place.

There would be false alarms, planes and ships passing too far away. If she withstood the attacks of helplessness and didn't give up, something good would happen. She would find land or be picked up. By now *Childhood II* must certainly have been sighted. The search for her had unquestionably begun.

She went on looking, though there was nothing to see but sameness. The ocean was telling her how small she was.

Around four o'clock came the thump, thump of fish striking the raft with their tails. She knelt at the edge of an outside log and peered straight down.

Below her were mobs of brilliantly colored fish. They were near the surface and she could see them clearly. She lowered her right hand into the water. The fish fled, but presently were back. She wiggled her fingers like live bait, luring them. She singled out the biggest fish and tried to catch them when they swam close. Her hand moved more slowly in the water than in the air. She failed again and again.

Toward sunset the fish suddenly darted off in a burst of motion and color.

Lisa yanked her hand from the water, knowing.

Ten yards out a shark's fin cut the surface. The savage hunter swam lazily, pleasing itself.

Heart pounding, Lisa squirmed back from the edge of the raft and grasped the center handgrip.

The shark continued its leisurely pace, looping around and around. It seemed to be sizing up this strange new form of prey, content not to rush things.

Suddenly its path straightened. The fin narrowed to its lead edge like a rifle swinging behind its muzzle.

Lisa tightened her grasp on the handgrip. She braced herself as best she could and waited.

The expected jolt did not occur. The shark slid by, scarcely two yards from the side of the raft. It glided on, cruised through a shortened loop, and, putting on speed, sliced in again.

This time it came up out of the water—ten feet of doll eyes, teeth, and terror.

After three more passes, each a little bolder, a little closer, it cruised off.

By tomorrow, when hunger turned cruising into killing, it would be back.

With friends, Lisa thought.

Chapter 3

The Island

Rain fell early on the second day. Although barely more than a sprinkle, it wet Lisa's lips and tongue and relieved her thirst.

The clouds hurried on, chased by a wind from the east that roughened the surface. The raft seemed to race forward. It bounced and rolled but always righted itself as though it had been born in the water.

Several times that morning Lisa thought she had spied land. The distant gray spots, phantoms of her imagination, appeared and disappeared regularly, unmercifully.

Late in the afternoon a funny-looking sea gull flew over, squawking above the noises of waves and wind. It swung back and forth, writing its message on the sky: *land is near.* To be sure, the gull, if gull it be, was a sorry, dull-colored little creature. But to Lisa nothing with wings ever fitted better the title "bird of paradise."

She wiped salt spray from her lashes and squinted at the horizon.

Land . . . she saw land! Directly ahead . . . an island! Would it vanish, too?

She tested it by glancing away. When she looked back, it was still there: two cliffs connected by low-lying ground.

How had she missed seeing it sooner?

The sun must be getting to me, she thought.

Now if only the wind held. Her existence depended on the wind helping the westward current.

As the distance shrank, the color of the land changed from brown to green. Lisa could almost hear the rustle of palm trees, taste coconut milk, smell flowers.

Presently real and less welcome details stood out like special effects in a movie set. Even with a wind at her back, coming ashore would not be easy.

At the northern end of the island the ocean crashed against one of the cliffs. At the southern end, breakers foamed over a rim of rocks at the foot of the second, lower cliff. Between, glowing beautifully in the dying fires of day, lay safety—a small beach.

She was getting ready to swim to it when a black fin knifed in front of her. Three more trailed the raft.

Sharks.

Right on time, she thought with a shudder.

Gaining the shore ceased to be just a matter of

dodging the unpursuing cliff or rocks. The sharks forced a terrible choice: try to swim through them or remain on the raft.

She knew the ways of the sea against an island. The current splits near the shore and comes together on the far side. If she chose the raft, she'd drift around the island and might eventually be swept north by the Gulf Stream, a death sentence of a trip.

She put it to herself in simplest terms: hunger and thirst versus the sharks. She picked the sharks.

By now she had nearly enough adrenaline coursing to sprint on top of the water. Fingers trembling, she tucked the Swiss Army knife, longest blade opened, into her belt.

She fumbled off her shoes and held one in each hand.

Did sharks eat leather?

She was about to find out.

Seventy or eighty yards offshore, the raft turned. It had caught the split current and was drifting left.

Lisa waited as long as she dared and threw a shoe.

The shark in front of her seemed to take forever before darting toward the bait.

Lisa threw the other shoe at the sharks behind her, and went into the water.

She should have liked to sneak in feet first. Sharp chest-ripping rocks might lie just below the surface. But she needed the head start of a dive.

She flattened out in midair and was swimming. There was no holding back, no pacing herself, no

13

bothering with form. Her arms and legs thrashed with all the strength in them.

She became aware of her skin. She felt every inch of it, felt its thinness coating her abdomen, her breasts, the soles of her feet—skin the sharks would pierce like paper.

She lifted her head to breathe and saw the beach squarely ahead of her.

Forty yards to go . . . thirty . . .

She was slowing. The crosscurrent battled her every stroke.

Twenty-five yards now . . . twenty . . .

Her lungs were burning and her arms were giving out. She didn't see how she was going to get away—and then the bottom rose up and met her with surprising suddenness. She had passed over a ledge separating the deep water from the slope of the shallows. Only crabs and snails could follow her now!

She struggled to all fours and flung herself onto the sand. Lacy fringes of surf flowed and ebbed delicately around her feet. She lay panting painfully, too tired to move another inch up the beach. All that mattered was that she had cheated the sharks of dinner. She was alive!

She fought the urge to doze off where she lay. Come on, she thought with a sailor's extra sense of caution. Get up. Get out of sight.

With the last of her strength she stumbled into the jungle bordering the beach and fell numbly into sleep.

She was awakened by a morning bright enough for two suns and as silent as a free fall. It was ten minutes past eleven. She had slept longer than she had ever slept in her life.

She glanced around, remembering where she was—on an island she didn't know existed. To her left was something that made her forget her thirst and hunger: a sawed-off tree. No, several, she discovered.

Cut trees meant humans. But who were they? The island was not on her charts.

"Hello."

A girl dressed in sandals, white shorts, and a white T-shirt stood on the sand not far from where Lisa had slept.

"My name is Amelia," she said with a small, lonely smile.

Chapter 4

Amelia

The two girls stared at each other.

Lisa's first reaction was that an island somewhere in the Atlantic Ocean was a terribly wrong place to find a child.

Her second was that Amelia would bloom into a beauty. In a few years she would have her ring of admirers, boys who couldn't stop gawking long enough to say hello.

She had fine cheekbones, freckles, full lips, and a short straight nose—features touched with a boyish charm. Her flaxen hair was pulled back sternly over her ears and twisted into a bun on the left side. She was slightly built, with slim long arms and legs that suggested she would grow tall for a woman.

Lisa guessed her age as about ten. Yet, she seemed much older. In some way or another, Amelia had learned to fit the extraordinary—such as discovering a stranger on the beach—into the ordinary run of her life.

"What's your name?" she inquired.

"Lisa Maddock. I could use a drink of water."

"Come with me," Amelia said politely. "It's not far."

They followed a footpath through masses of undergrowth and queerly shaped palm and hardwood trees.

Amelia led, hurrying along eagerly. She turned once and saw Lisa falling behind.

"Are you all right?" she called.

"Just stiff. I haven't done much walking in a couple of days."

Amelia slowed. The path forked and she went right. Presently they came to a clearing. In the center stood a well.

Amelia flipped a lever and tossed down a wooden bucket. The spool and crank spun, letting out rope till the bucket hit with a delicious splash.

Lisa bent over the brickwork circling the well. She seized the bucket when it rose within arm's length.

She allowed herself five careful swallows and no more, though she could have drunk the bucket dry. The rest of the water she poured over her head.

Amelia was about to drop the empty bucket into the well again. Lisa stopped her.

"That's enough," she said. "I don't want to bloat."

"Are you hungry, Miss Maddock?" Amelia asked. "There's plenty of food in the iceboxes."

"I'm Lisa, and, no thanks. A coconut will do me for now."

Hunger was biting in her, but her curiosity was stronger. Iceboxes, as Amelia had quaintly put it, meant houses and people. Lisa did not care to share her. She wanted the girl to herself a bit longer. She had questions.

Keeping Amelia in sight, she walked to several coconuts lying in a nest of weeds. She found one that sloshed upon being shaken. With her knife she peeled off the brown husk, cracked the shell against a rock, tasted the milk, and dug out the white meat.

Amelia had been staring at her all the while. When she saw that Lisa noticed, her cheeks colored with a well-bred blush.

Quickly she said, "How did you get here, Lisa?"

"By accident. I fell off a sailboat and hitched a ride on a raft." She described her two days adrift, the fish she did not catch, the sea gull, and the race against the sharks.

"I had an accident, too," Amelia said solemnly. "They say I had a dizzy spell and fainted."

"You're all right now?"

"I think so." The accident still troubled her, for she changed the subject abruptly. "I have a mystery barn. No one can go there without me. Would you like to see it?" She didn't stay around for an answer, but struck off into the jungle.

Lisa fell in behind her.

They had traveled scarcely a minute when a barn loomed through the trees.

"I play here all the time," Amelia said. "I can do anything I want to. You have to see what's inside!"

A foghorn blasted twice in the distance.

"Oh, that's lunch," Amelia grumbled. "I must go."

"You'll be back, I hope?" Lisa said anxiously.

"You're not coming with me?"

"No, I'll wait for you here."

"Can I bring you something to eat?"

Lisa thought of asking her to bring some salt to replace what she'd sweated on the raft. But Amelia might be seen snitching it.

"I'm okay," Lisa said.

She wished she'd been around ten-year-old girls more and learned how to talk to them. She could not think of a clever way to ask Amelia what she was doing on the island.

Clumsily she said, "Do you like games?"

"I like boys' games. Grandma says they're not fitting for girls. She says when she was my age the most she did was roll a hoop in the public square."

"We can play a game," Lisa said. "It's called our secret."

"What is our secret?"

"Me," Lisa said. "Can you keep me a secret? I'd like to meet your folks when I'm wide awake. I wouldn't want to fall asleep at the table."

Amelia looked at her guardedly, as though she knew she wasn't being told all she needed to know.

20

"The fact is, I'm awfully tired," Lisa hastened on. "While you're at lunch, I'll take a nap."

She drooped her dark, curly head to one side and shut her eyes and snored like a grizzly in winter.

The clowning served better than words. Amelia giggled.

"This evening I'll meet your folks," Lisa said. "How about it?"

Amelia moved her shoulders. "I won't tell anyone you're here," she promised. Her voice lowered. "But they're not my folks."

With that, she disappeared into the jungle.

Chapter 5

The Mystery Barn

Amelia had made no sound at all. The jungle folded behind her, and she seemed never to have existed.

The barn where she played was still there. Her "mystery" barn.

It looked like a large lean-to with walls, owing to the front and back parts of the roof being of unequal pitches and lengths. The short side in front slanted sharply down to the double doors of the entrance. The long side in the rear slanted less sharply and covered three-quarters of the barn, ending close to the ground.

Lisa saw no hint of mystery about the barn save its forsaken look. Tall trees grew close to the walls, as if the jungle were returning, taking back the ground that had been cleared by man. A broken treetop poked through the roof.

Lisa pulled open the double doors as far as the trees let her. Daylight crept in.

She caught her breath in surprise.

An antique car—a two-seat black runabout—was parked on the earthen floor. The absence of bumpers, top, and doors dated it well before World War I. Yet, it appeared to be in original condition.

Something about the little car made her feel as if she'd got into a dream.

She pressed the thin tires. They were hard with air, and worn.

Behind the seats was a polished cylinder, the gas tank. She unscrewed the cap and stuck a finger in.

The tank was nearly full.

She paced off the width of the car. She paced off the narrow opening between the double doors. The car was six inches wider.

The measurements were spooky. They added up to an unshatterable fact: the car had been there before the barn. And unless the trees blocking the doors from opening all the way were uprooted, the car had to stay where it was.

Actually, the doors didn't matter. Where could anyone go for a spin? How long would the tires and that snazzy black paint job last crashing through the bushes and trees?

A better question was, Who had abandoned the barn and the car to the jungle?

Collectors of old cars, Lisa decided, are even crazier than sailors.

She remembered the craziest—a man in Utah who kept a 1903 curved-dash Oldsmobile in his living room.

The difference troubled her. The car in Utah was a showpiece. The car in front of her had gas in the tank and air in the tires, as if it were used every day.

She turned her attention to the other old machine in the barn, a steam tractor. With its long boiler and upright funnel, it looked like a tiny locomotive. Lumps of earth clung to the metal tread of the rear wheels.

Behind the tractor were antique tools, including a black gum plowshare, dozens of oak pegs, and three saws with apple handles. Like the car and tractor, the tools appeared to be in ready-to-use shape.

Off to her right stood a tree. Lisa at first thought it must be artificial. It was not.

The tree had all its branches and leaves up to the roof. What's more, many of the leaves were green. The smaller branches, which had grown high on the tree and had broken as the tree pierced the roof, lay near the base of the trunk.

Lisa peered up at the hole, trying to make sense out of the senseless.

She started getting scared.

"I'm back," Amelia called. "I brought you sandals and a peach. No one saw me."

"Your mystery barn sure beats me," Lisa said as

she munched the peach. "The car is all gassed up and no place to go. And the tree growing in darkness has some green leaves."

Amelia giggled. "Slope your barn 'gainst northern blast, and heat of day is made to last."

"Is that a riddle?"

"Yes, it's not what is *in* the barn. The mystery *is* the barn," Amelia exclaimed. "It's built for snow."

"We're too far south for snow," Lisa remarked. "It hasn't snowed here since the Ice Age."

"My friend Mary Anne Denton lives on a farm in Atcheson. Her father's barn is just like this one," Amelia said.

Lisa wasn't following.

"I'll show you," Amelia said.

She took hold of Lisa's sleeve and tugged her out of the barn and around to the back.

"See there," she said, pointing to the three feet between the low end of the rear roof and the ground. "Mary Anne's father banks this space with hay, cornstalks, or leaves mixed with sod. Then the snow can pile up over the roof from there so the wind doesn't reach the inside of the barn. Don't you see?"

"No," Lisa said. "I'm not a farmer. Away from a deck I'm easily lost."

"Well, look for yourself." Amelia pointed to the long slope of the rear roof. "Slope your barn 'gainst northern blast," she recited again. "Now do you see?"

"No,"

"Oh, Lisa! This kind of barn is built so the back faces toward the north wind. It doesn't!"

She was right. The low back of the barn faced west.

A barn in the tropics built for snowy whiteouts up north. With the goof in the direction it faced. There had to be a simple explanation, of course.

Lisa considered the spot in the roof where the tree had broken through. The top part of the trunk, some ten feet in length, lay in the underbrush nearby.

She knelt and examined it. All its branches had been sheared off. She had seen the branches, with many leaves still green, lying inside the barn.

So the time was fixed. The ten-foot trunk above the roof had broken off recently.

It took an effort to add up what she was seeing.

A tree breaking through a roof would not grow another ten feet before snapping off.

The sweat on her palms turned cold as understanding stole through her.

"Do you know how the tree broke?" she asked Amelia offhandedly.

"It was like this when I started to play here," Amelia replied. "They say it broke growing through the roof."

"I don't believe that," Lisa said.

Amelia regarded her questioningly.

Lisa considered withholding what she knew was almost certainly the fact. Spare her, don't scare her.

27

Then she thought, Tell the truth if you want to be told the truth about the island.

She said, "It looks to me as if the barn fell from the sky."

Chapter 6

≈

A Face Remembered

Amelia did not frighten.

Instead she asked gravely, "Can a barn really fall from the sky?"

"I don't know how."

"You were teasing?"

"I wish I were."

"Yes, you were teasing!"

Lisa shook her head. "I'm sorry, there are a lot of things that I can't explain."

"Like what?"

"All sorts of things. Why don't we sit down and talk." She weighed her next words carefully. "The old car looks comfortable."

She held out a tanned hand. Trustingly, Amelia clasped it. They walked into the barn.

"You drive," Lisa said.

Amelia mounted the driver's seat with a tomboy's

swift, untamed grace. She clenched both fists around the steering wheel. "Why did you call this an *old* car?"

Lisa had planted the question. Nevertheless, the response came back to her as a time warp spilling out of a young girl's mouth. Chilling.

"Dunno," she said, holding her voice steady. "I guess I use 'old' as a term for a lot of cute things. I haven't seen a car as cute as this in a while. Have you?"

"My uncle has one just like it," Amelia said. "He bought it new in January. He keeps it in a shed when it snows."

The mystery of how an old car could be bought new in January matched the mystery of the barn. In that mix-up of time, Amelia's face and name suddenly found a place in Lisa's memory. Face and name matched the adult Amelia, the world-famous Amelia, the dead Amelia. Lisa had seen black-and-white photographs of her and her airplanes in books and magazines.

She studied the Amelia beside her out of the corner of her eye and wondered if two days on the raft had left her dancing mad.

"Do you like to drive automobiles?" she asked.

Amelia giggled. "You're silly, I'm too small. But it's fun coming here and playing motorist."

The next question burned on Lisa's tongue. "Do you like airplanes?"

"I saw an airplane last year on my ninth birthday. It was in a field at the Iowa State Fair. Daddy bought us another pony ride and paper hats so we'd go with him and watch it fly."

"Who is 'we'?"

"Muriel and me. She's my little sister."

"Did you enjoy the airplane?"

"Oh, it was all right," Amelia said. "You couldn't get close, though."

Lisa's throat tightened. "What did it look like?"

"It had two wings and lots of wires," Amelia answered. "There was a man wearing goggles sitting between the wings. He had his feet on a crossbar. Behind him was an engine with a propeller."

She had described a plane from the pioneer days of aviation.

"I'll bet you'd like to fly when you grow up," Lisa said.

"If somebody would teach me," Amelia replied. "I'd fly all the way from Iowa to Kansas to see Grandma Otis."

"Is that what you want to be, a pilot?" Lisa inquired softly.

"Aviatrix, you mean? Golly, no. I like horses better than airplanes. I ride every chance I get."

Lisa had been delaying, but she could delay no more. It had to come out, even if the answer threatened all reason.

Now, she thought.

She tried to make the question sound spur-of-the-moment. But her tongue seemed to have thickened and the words barely squeezed out.

"You never told me your last name."

"Earhart," Amelia replied sweetly.

The name pounded at Lisa, though it hardly came as a surprise. Quite the opposite. She knew it was coming even as she dreaded hearing it.

It fell upon her in a grapeshot of facts and images: Amelia Earhart, the first woman to fly across the ocean alone; Amelia Earhart, the envy of every female and the heartthrob of every male; Amelia Earhart, tall, courageous, beautiful; Amelia Earhart, missing forever while on a flight over the Pacific Ocean, July 1937.

Keep a grip, Lisa thought desperately, for there was no possibility of a mistake. The ocean had cast her ashore on an island that somehow, in some way, had lost nearly a century. Or where time was running backward.

I'm sharing a day in the childhood of a woman who died long before I was born, she thought.

She let out breath. She hadn't realized she was holding it.

Next to her was the girl who had already grown up to become the most famous female pilot in history. Once she was a shyly smiling, bobbed-haired, all-American heroine from Kansas with a deep, deep hunger for fame.

"Lisa, is something wrong?"

"It's very warm in here."

"It's always cooler on the beach," Amelia said, and hopped to the ground. "Let's go there."

She closed the garage doors by herself, refusing Lisa's offer of help. "I can do it," she announced, as if speaking for Amelia the adult as well.

Clearly she was ignorant of her future. She did not know. She had either been lifted above her later years, or been whisked through them too fast for anything to stick. She was pure ten-year-old. As she walked, she poked under leaves and complained. She hadn't found a single arrowhead on the island to add to her collection.

At the beach they talked about her life in Atcheson and in Des Moines, where her family had moved "last year." Dusk glazed the tops of the trees when Lisa finally got around to it.

"You told me you had an accident and fainted," she said. "Exactly what happened?"

"I was walking on stilts in our backyard," Amelia replied. "Muriel and I made them ourselves. They say that's when I fainted."

"You remember nothing else?"

"Nope," Amelia said. She had removed her sandals and was rubbing tracks in the sand with her bare heels. "I woke up in the hospital here. They said I'd been unconscious a lot, but I was all right. They want me to rest some more in the ocean air. Then I can go home."

"Who told you all this? Who are 'they'?"

"The doctors."

"Do you like them?"

"They don't act like Dr. Golden back home."

"What do you mean?"

"I never did feel sick, and I don't think they know what to do for me." She tried to smile, but the delight had gone out of her face. "I'm like a pet."

"Like a pet they're studying?"

"Yes!" she cried. "Oh, Lisa, that's how I feel!"

Lisa stood and brushed the sand from her shorts.

She knew about the half-grown Amelia Earhart. Now she had to know about the others on the island. They would find her sooner or later. There was no point in hiding anymore.

"It's time for me," she said, "to meet your doctors."

Chapter 7

The Village

Amelia forged along a trail worn into the curving centerline of the island. After traveling about twenty minutes, she halted.

"Here we are," she said, and pointed. "I live in that big house."

Ahead of them rose a curious village.

Dirt paths wound among the houses like flat brown creepers. The yards, both front and back, were choked with jungle scrub. It was impossible to tell where one property line ended and another began.

All the houses were built of wood, and painted white. They ranged in size from tiny cottages to three-story gabled mansions. The architecture was a patchwork of New England, Creole, Bahamian, and Victorian. Lisa had sailed past similar houses in the Florida Keys.

Rising like a vapor from the roofs and windows and porches was the same out-of-place quality that she had felt at Amelia's mystery barn. She saw the village—a community without storefronts or streets—as though peering into a looking glass. Everything seemed nearly normal, nearly real.

It was not the houses themselves that were so curious but how they were laid out. Instead of forming neat rows, they faced in every direction, as if they had been built somewhere else and dumped willy-nilly on the island. Or grown from house seeds scattered by the hand of a careless giant. Or floated down from the sky.

Amelia bounded up the steps and onto the veranda of the big house.

"This is the hospital," she said, tugging on the screen door.

Lisa reached out a helping hand.

"I can manage, thank you," Amelia declared, her independence flaring. She gave the stuck door an extra hard yank and sprang it open. "My room is on the second floor. I have my own balcony."

As Lisa started inside, she noticed the plaque by the top hinge of the door:

HISTORIC HOME

As she was pondering what committee had awarded the plaque, a male voice called.

"Amelia, is that you?"

36

"Yes, I have a visitor."

A door in the large center hall swung ajar. A butterball of a man in a white jacket and trousers inched out. He gaped at Lisa in astonishment.

"I fell off a sailboat," Lisa said quickly. "I was delivering her to the owner in Saint Thomas in the Virgin Islands. Amelia has helped me."

The butterball continued to gape with unlessened astonishment.

"I fell off a sailboat," Lisa repeated. "That's the truth. I swam ashore yesterday evening. My name is Lisa Maddock and I live in Miami, Florida. I'd be grateful if you'd call the Coast Guard in Key West."

A hairy hand, too large for the speechless butterball in the doorway, grasped the edge of the door. The door swung wider, bringing into view a lanky young man with a beardless, craggy face.

He greeted Lisa with a tired, kindly smile.

"What do you think, Abe?" the butterball said nervously.

"A visitor is Dr. Freemont's concern," said Abe. His voice had the long-drawn, raspy drawl of an actor playing the role of a frontiersman. "Conduct our new friend to the office, Elliot. We can finish the checkers later."

Lisa looked hard to be certain. Abe was like a three-dimensional photograph onto which a frock coat, a high hat, and a beard begged to be penciled.

"Why don't *you* take me to the office, Abe?" Lisa was about to say.

The thought came too late. The young Abe had already bowed from his splendid height and turned into the room. The opportunity to have an American immortal fulfill a small request had flown.

"I'll take Lisa to the office," Amelia declared.

"No," Elliot the butterball said. "Best you stay here."

"I don't think that's fair," Amelia objected with an injured expression. "I found her!"

"I don't make the rules," Elliot said. "Dr. Freemont does. Now off to your room and don't borrow trouble."

"Go without me, then!" Amelia said peevishly. "But Lisa doesn't have to do anything she doesn't want to!" And having lost the little passage-at-arms, she grudgingly mounted the stairs.

"She won't ever be the kind for lacy gowns and satin bows, will she?" Elliot said. He laid a pudgy hand against Lisa's shoulder blade and ushered her out the door.

The office building was a rambling mansion of many shapes—towers, bay windows, porches, and wraparound veranda all grandly trimmed with gingerbread tracery. Elliot's knock was answered by a handsome, unsmiling woman cleanly uniformed in white.

Elliot introduced Lisa as a "shipwreck." The woman gaped with something stronger than astonishment.

She pulled Elliot inside.

A low, excited exchange followed between the pair behind the closed door. Lisa could make out none of it save the oft-repeated name, Freemont.

Elliot came out, bade Lisa wait, and took to his heels, obviously relieved to be rid of any responsibility.

A minute went by . . . then another, and another.

The knob clinked and the front door grated and opened all the way.

"Dr. Freemont will receive you," the woman said, stepping aside.

Chapter 8

An Unusual Dinner

The room to which the cold-looking woman brought Lisa was remarkable for its lack of luxury and comfort. The only sticks of furniture were two straight-backed wooden chairs and a desk.

Behind the desk sat a slender man of about forty-five. He had graying hair and a lurking hint of uncommon energy. His cat green eyes shone with the light of someone who knows places that no one else knows.

He got to his feet and glided gracefully toward Lisa with hand outstretched.

"How nice to meet you, Lisa Maddock," he said. "I am Dr. Preston Freemont."

Lisa shook the outstretched hand. It was as firm as her own.

"I was about to have dinner," Freemont continued. "But we cannot talk in the mess hall. We shall dine here in the office, just we two, and have our little chat in private."

Freemont's manner was put-on smooth, from the overdone handshake to the eye contact that lasted seconds too long.

Something is bothering him. Something about me, Lisa thought uncomfortably.

Freemont turned to the woman. "You may serve us straightaway, Hilda. Our young guest must be hungry as a wolf. Do you have a favorite dish, Miss Maddock?"

"Whatever is easy."

"Anything is easy. We take pride in that. And you'll find our food doesn't suffer from the trip."

"Lobster, then," Lisa said, testing.

"How do you like it?" Freemont asked with a hint of amusement. "Broiled? Steamed? Boiled?"

"Broiled is fine."

"You heard, Hilda? Lobster, broiled."

The woman nodded. "Very good," she said, and withdrew.

"A loyal soul, Hilda," Freemont said. "She is a first-rate mathematician who can whip up a banquet, let us say, at the lift of your eyebrow. You shall see." He sat down behind the desk and signaled Lisa to the only other chair. "I read about you in last week's *Miami Times-Journal.* I try to keep informed. You're the youngest professional skipper in Florida, are you not?"

"So people tell me," Lisa said. "I was delivering a

sloop, *Childhood II,* to her owner in Saint Thomas when I went overboard. I'm not sure where I am."

"You're safe," Freemont said, and shifted the conversation. "You must love the sea."

"I was raised on the water," Lisa replied. "My dad is the senior dockmaster for the Port of Miami. As long as I can remember, I was always scouting the beaches for shells and driftwood, or studying the creatures that live in shallow pools."

"I, too, grew up in Florida," Freemont said. "In Melbourne Beach. When I was eleven, my father bought me a skiff. One day I sailed out of sight of land and made a discovery. The sea and sky and time are kin. The skiff and I were newcomers. Only we were aging."

He leaned forward and peered at Lisa.

"I have been a student of time and the sea and the sky ever since," he said.

A knock sounded on the door. It was Hilda.

She laid upon the desk a metal restaurant tray with napkins, silverware, cups, a coffee pitcher, and two large dishes with plate covers to keep them hot.

When she lifted the plate covers, Lisa looked upon the two biggest lobsters she had ever seen. Twelve pounds each if an ounce.

She dug in hungrily.

Her enjoyment, however, was marred by an unsettling habit of Freemont's. Whenever she glanced up, she caught him watching her keenly.

"You don't find a lobster this size too tough?" he inquired.

"Not at all," Lisa said, the last bite still in her cheek, and scowled.

"Something is wrong?"

"Lobsters in this part of the world don't have claws," Lisa answered. "Maine lobsters have claws. These lobsters have claws. Therefore, these lobsters are Maine lobsters."

"Indeed?"

"Yet, they're *fresh* lobsters. They weren't fished from a freezer. I've eaten enough of them to know."

"What is the point?"

"You're fooling with me," Lisa said. "You want me to think that in a few minutes you had a fresh lobster dinner for two prepared and brought a couple of thousand miles to a tropical island."

"An instant Maine lobster dinner in the tropics is a puzzle to you," Freemont said. "Just as you, Miss Maddock—I confess it—are a puzzle to me."

"Call me Lisa."

"Let it be Lisa and Preston, shall we? Quite frankly, Lisa, I can bring a lobster from Maine or a steak from Texas faster than you can snap your fingers. But you can't have reached this island after falling overboard. The truth, if you please. How did you get here?"

"Why not the same way the lobsters did?"

Freemont grinned. "You have a quick wit, and you don't scare easily, young lady," he allowed. "A fresh

Maine lobster, broiled and served within minutes of the ordering! Such a feat would have upset the appetite of the average girl—if she were sufficiently clever to think on it."

A motor roared overhead.

"Probably a search plane hunting for me," Lisa said.

"A waste of time," Freemont stated. "The island is invisible."

"I saw it."

"That is the puzzle. Tell me, how did you get here?"

"I rode a raft close to the beach and swam ashore."

"This raft," Freemont said thinly. "Was it made of logs held together by pegs and vines, with carved handgrips on top and bottom?"

"Yes."

Freemont sighed deeply. His face relaxed. Lisa had never seen such an expression of relief in all her life.

"The logs came from the trees growing here. That is why you saw the island," Freemont said. "Being on the raft was like being on the island. Once within the island's time zone, you could leave the raft and swim ashore, touch the sand, hear the wind rustle the leaves."

"I'm missing something," Lisa said. "What's the island's time zone?"

"This island sank into the ocean more than a million years ago," Freemont said. "I brought it into the present, exactly as it was on its last days above the water. Naturally, I had to bring in some things from the world of today."

Lisa stamped her foot. "I couldn't have done this if I'd grounded my sailboat on the shore?"

"You'd have sailed right through the island without seeing it." Freemont dabbed at his mouth with a napkin. "I have done," he declared, "what science says cannot be done. I have brought objects and people out of the past without leaving holes that change the present. Trust me on that."

"I trust anyone who feeds me," Lisa quipped, forcing a smile. "I even trust a restaurant cook—unless he's skinny."

Freemont borrowed the smile and added a sly twinkle. "We are eating lobsters caught more than a hundred years ago," he said. "They are straight from Danny's Seafood Café in Maine. The time was seven-thirty-seven in the evening of February tenth. In the year eighteen hundred and ninety-one. A waiter named Lars Bergstrom brought an order of broiled lobsters to a couple at table five. It takes only the smallest part of a second to beam the tray from Bergstrom's hand to Hilda's."

Lisa didn't bat an eye at Freemont's words. Half a day on the island had conditioned her to take seriously any claim, regardless of how far-fetched it seemed. She was almost beginning to feel at home with the miraculous.

"Sounds like you have a paradise here," she said. "But life for everyone isn't all fun and lobsters, is it?"

"You mean Amelia? Come, come, she is a little girl, skipping back and forth between fantasy and reality, full of accepting. She'll adjust."

"I don't mean Amelia," Lisa said. "I mean whoever built the raft. He was trying to escape, wasn't he?"

Chapter 9

The Man Who Built
the Raft

"The man who built the raft," Freemont said, "was George Washington."

"You brought him to this island?"

Freemont chuckled. "You are a cool one, Lisa Maddock. You ought to be plucking at your throat and shaking in every limb, or regarding me as if I were some mad scientist leering over a rack of bubbling test tubes."

"I saw an Abraham Lincoln of about thirty in the hospital half an hour ago," Lisa said, scarcely believing her own words. "You know I made friends with Amelia Earhart. She died a grown woman before World War II. The little freckle-faced Amelia Earhart hasn't guessed the truth. She thinks she's recovering from a fainting spell—back around nineteen hundred and eight."

"She'll be able to handle it," Freemont said. "Thank make-believe. It's a child's preparation for the fantastic. She'll—"

"George Washington," Lisa interrupted, "must have understood what had happened to him."

"He understood. He built the raft to escape."

"He never made it, did he?"

A flush rose to Freemont's cheeks. "He escaped, in a manner of speaking. He was the first person I brought from the past . . . the responsibility is mine."

"What happened?"

"An error in mathematics, in the fusing of time and motion and space. Let it go at that. So with the next one, Amelia Earhart, I overcorrected. I took Washington from the past too late, a couple of weeks before his death as a man of sixty-seven. Earhart was snatched too soon, when she was only ten." Freemont clapped the arm of his chair in a gesture of regret. "I hadn't yet perfected the method of bringing people from the past, or treating them. That is different now."

"I can't imagine what it was like for George Washington," Lisa muttered.

"Try unbearable," Freemont said stonily. "He uttered little moans and drew up his feet and clawed at his temples whenever he thought he was alone. We let him roam the island freely until we decided what to do."

"And you decided?"

"Nothing. He removed himself from any decision

of ours. He built the raft down on the beach with a handsaw, mallet, and chisel, old as he was. In his boyhood he was good at cutting down trees, or so the legend goes. But I couldn't let him set off. He wouldn't have lasted two days under this sun."

Freemont sipped his coffee, set the cup down, and stirred in a drop more cream.

"During a storm last month," he said, "I had the raft hauled out to sea. I ordered it sunk, but the high winds and waves obviously prevented that. I was not told."

The disobedience still rankled. He glared out the window before going on.

"Washington was to believe the storm had carried the raft away. He never learned it was missing. He died that night. He was born in the eighteenth century and lived the final two weeks of his life over again in the present. His hours simply ran out the night of the storm."

"Since the raft was built with trees from the island, how did it remain visible and real after going beyond the time zone?" Lisa asked.

"Blame a kink in the time-space contact. It is being repaired. Meanwhile, the raft will be beamed to the island before it is found. Would you like me to explain the kink?"

"You know it won't do any good," Lisa stammered with a note of sadness. "Washington's raft saved my life. I'll never be able to thank him."

"You can if I let you," Freemont replied. "I may bring him back. As a young man."

Lisa stood up, deliberately turning her back on Freemont. She took two steps toward the window. Her heart was beating so wildly that she was afraid to go farther.

George Washington, after dying twice as an old man, might be brought back to the island in his prime. What for? What need had Freemont of him—and of Amelia Earhart and Abraham Lincoln?

She stared at the village.

Were there more leaders of another day, alive again, dwelling beneath those roofs?

Freemont had a purpose for invading the past. Clearly it wasn't to turn the island into a living museum with a slick-haired pitchman barking, "Step right up, folks! See Abraham Lincoln for a dollar and a half!"

Whatever Freemont's purpose, Lisa had seen enough to believe he could achieve it. The greatest men and women of history were as primitive as mushrooms dotting a meadow compared to a man who made yesterday catch up with today.

"Frankly," Freemont said, "beaming a human can be less trouble sometimes than beaming a building. I have to target historic buildings at night, when they are empty—the tourists have left and the guides and staff have gone home. I can't risk taking a house with someone inside."

"And Amelia's barn? Where did it come from?"

"Pennsylvania, in nineteen nine. I let Hilda practice on buildings. You may have noticed she missed a perfect landing with the barn. She set it down in the clearing six feet off center."

"Right on top of a tree," Lisa added.

"Hilda does better with smaller objects like the lobsters, the car and tractor beamed in to amuse Amelia, or the well near the barn. As you may have guessed, Hilda is my wife."

Lisa hadn't guessed. The news startled her. Hilda's work with beaming barely earned a passing grade. Nonetheless, Freemont loyally allowed her to continue. Suddenly he became a bit more of a feeling human being, a bit less of an awe-striking figure molded by almost unlimited power.

She pressed on with her questions. "Don't you leave empty spaces where your buildings had stood?"

"The barn is still in Pennsylvania. All the other buildings on the island are where they were built. I guarantee you, I have not bent a blade of grass."

"The buildings are both there and here?"

"Certainly."

"You did the same with Washington and Lincoln and Amelia?"

Freemont gave a superior tilt to his head before replying.

Chapter 10

Time out of Time

"The past is unchanged," Freemont said. "Washington and Amelia were left at the spot from which they were taken. Washington was riding Pudge, a bay stallion. Amelia was in her backyard, playing on homemade stilts with her sister."

"Could I understand how you do it?"

"There is no fast explanation, I'm afraid. But look at it this way, Lisa. Nothing is at rest. Not the pyramids, not Mount Rushmore, not the White House. Everything on earth moves in time even when appearing to stand still in space. Slow the movement down to a crawl, and what do things look like? They look rather like a series of separate sections, like frames in a movie film. Does that help you?"

"You somehow snip a frame from the past and bring it into the present?" Lisa ventured.

"An excellent description, 'snip,'" Freemont

answered. "During an instant too brief to describe, the before-and-after frames in the past fuse and the past becomes continuous once more. The single, snipped-out frame is spliced into the present, where it bonds instantly."

"Surely someone might see the frame removed," Lisa objected. "That's all it would take to change the future forever."

"The loss of one frame can barely be noticed. I snipped Abraham Lincoln while he was walking outside his law office in Springfield. The lone sign was that he jerked slightly. The stolen frame made him appear to lose his footing for a split second, as if he had started to—but didn't—stumble. If someone noticed him jerk, what was there to suspect? That a split second of Abe Lincoln had been snatched into the future?"

Freemont's right hand lifted. He waved at the village. "Join us," he said.

"Join what?" Lisa exclaimed, taken aback. "I don't understand how you do it, much less why."

"Is this earth a good place?" Freemont asked.

"It's better than none."

"You think I plan to save this earth by stocking it with the best leaders from the past?"

"Something like it."

"Look here," Freemont said. "I have not mastered the future—or the human spirit. How can you truly think it is within my power to save the world? I cannot. No one can."

"We can try. If we all put aside greed and pull together."

"My dear, innocent Lisa. This world wants to be left alone to kill itself. From polluted food and water. From the plagues of crime and drugs and politicians. From overheating."

A ghostlike grin played at the corners of his mouth.

"I cannot save this tortured old earth," he said. "So I shall start over."

Lisa tensed.

"What do you think of the year nineteen forty-six?" Freemont asked casually. "World War II had just ended. Nations were at peace. A good year, wouldn't you say?"

He did not wait for an answer, but continued:

"Take two hundred of history's greatest leaders. Train them and set them down in nineteen forty-six. With guidance, they can prevent the wrongs to come."

"No," Lisa objected. "No! To start over from nineteen forty-six would be murder. You'd wipe out the lives of the millions of people born since then and—"

She broke off, stunned.

"Y-you're not talking about this earth, about changing history *here,* are you?" she cried.

Freemont squinted at the accusation. "As I can move a person, or a building, or an island across space and time, so can I move a planet."

"Where?"

Freemont angled his chin so that it pointed toward the bottomless sky. "Up there."

"Snip a frame from earth of nineteen forty-six and plant it in outer space?"

"Snip an entire solar system as well. No one on New Earth will suspect a thing. I shall make of it a seat fit for angels."

"Our earth will spin on?"

"Right on course," Freemont said.

He licked his lips as though enjoying the taste of his words.

"But I can," he said, "also move objects and persons completely, leaving nothing behind. Like myself, my staff, and my two hundred."

Lisa remained silent, trying to pretend she was not shaken. She wished a big storm would howl through and blow away the last few days. A hurricane right then would have suited her just fine.

There was no wind. The air in the room hung heavy. All was still, and in the stillness it seemed to her that they were the only two people left in the world.

A church bell striking eight broke the spell. A bird twittered.

"When I headed the Federal Institute of Astrophysics," Freemont said, "I discovered how to tap into energy that can oppose time. I assembled and trained a staff in secret. Among their duties on New Earth will be to see that the leaders have husbands or wives of genius. Both groups will grow old and die. But their offspring will continue in their roles generation after generation."

Freemont eyed Lisa as though hoping the glimpse of New Earth tempted her.

"Soon my two hundred leaders will be ready," he said. "May I make it two hundred and one? I'll find a duty for you up there."

Why bother *asking*? Lisa thought. She countered with the question that had been swelling in her.

"Where do *you* fit into your New Earth?"

The temperature in the room seemed to drop below zero all at once.

Freemont raised his right fist and moved it in a restless, almost violent gesture. His eyes went cold and hard as winter stars.

"When you found the island, you became a danger, and so you must go where I go," he said in a tone that killed discussion. "Sleep on it. Tomorrow I want a yes answer."

Lisa left the room feeling as if she'd been tossed a hand grenade with the pin pulled.

Chapter 11

The Pact

Waiting outside the office was a huge bear of a man wearing the all-whites of Freemont's staff.

Specialist, strong-arm squad, Lisa thought.

"I'm Ross Barlow," the man said, and Lisa strained to hear a voice so gentle coming out of a man so large. "While you're with us here, I'll be your host."

Keeper, Lisa corrected silently, and wondered.

What if tonight or a week from tonight she hit upon a plan to sneak Amelia off the island? Could she get around the big man?

As it turned out, Barlow acted more like his voice than like his mountainous shoulders. He chattered pleasantly about the island's prehistoric wildlife as they walked toward a small cottage.

Lisa relaxed a notch. Violence, it appeared, was not Freemont's way. He was part scientist, part idealist. That was worth bearing in mind.

The cottage had a kitchen and two bedrooms with baths. "I'll be in the next room," Barlow said before locking Lisa's door. "I trust you'll find what you need. If you wish anything, call."

Lisa didn't call. She raised the shades.

The window in the bedroom and the one in the bathroom were guarded by iron bars.

And that, for tonight, shelved any idea of escaping.

She switched off the light and dropped wearily onto the four-poster bed, closed her eyes, and stared at her thoughts. Pictures of Amelia Earhart the child and Freemont's New Earth scrambled through her head. Never had she hung so close to the brink of the unreal.

It seemed she had scarcely dozed off when the squeak of wheels on the hardwood floor woke her.

Barlow had entered the sunlit bedroom, pushing a breakfast cart. "Have a good night?" he inquired with a servant's polite lack of personal concern.

"Pretty good, considering."

Barlow grinned. He laid white clothing over the back of an easy chair. "Dr. Freemont wishes to see you in his office in an hour."

He moved the dishes from the cart to the leaf table by the wall and departed, locking the door again.

Lisa glanced over the breakfast. There was plenty of it, but her stomach was in no mood for food. She got down a glass of orange juice and a bite of toast, emergency rations for the strength to face Freemont.

The white clothing Barlow had brought carried a fancy Miami label. The bathroom medicine cabinet housed a complete line of toiletries.

Shoplifting the past, Lisa decided, must be rather fun.

When she had showered and dressed in the whites, she rapped on the door. Barlow opened it carefully.

"I'm ready," Lisa said. "How do I look?"

Barlow stood in the doorway thinking it over.

"C'mon. How do I look?"

"Like a very pretty lady butcher."

"It's the hands," Lisa said. "Oh, well—"

Both chuckled.

In another place, in another day, Lisa thought, we might be good friends.

Walking to Freemont's office, they studiously avoided talk of what they saw and what they did not see.

They saw the buildings of the village. They saw several men and women dressed in whites hurrying along as if on some important mission.

They didn't see the others, who obviously were indoors. The giants of history, the leaders whom Freemont was stockpiling and training to guide New Earth, did not have the freedom of the island.

"How can Dr. Freemont take over New Earth

with only two hundred men and women?" Lisa asked.

"It can be done with fewer," Barlow replied, "if you have the tools of time. Think of your power over any-one if you know what he or she will do next every sec-ond of the day. Join that to the fact that nothing in anyone's past can be kept hidden, you follow me?"

"Sounds like blackmail," Lisa said.

"In an American courtroom, yes," Barlow agreed. "On an international scene, it is called diplo-macy."

He pressed his lips together, as if the little he'd given out was far too much. They walked to Freemont's front door without another word.

The time-master stood in his quick and correct manner as Lisa entered his office. His greeting was direct.

"Are you with me?"

Lisa shook her head. "Amelia is too young. I belong with my family and friends. We won't be any good to you. Leave us behind."

"Impossible."

"There have been other women fliers. Why must it be Amelia Earhart?"

"She is ideal."

"For what?"

"For bringing to New Earth equal rights for women."

"It'd be easier to time-steal some of this earth's equal-rights leaders and use them."

Freemont brushed aside the idea. "I want Amelia Earhart. I want her to prove that women can try things men have tried and still act like women. I want a role model, a *doer.*"

"I suppose you'll make her New Earth's first astronaut?"

"Oh, no, Lisa, I don't intend to limit her to one calling. Flying is out. Too dangerous. Besides, there have been better female pilots. But as a liberated woman, she laps the field."

"She went down in the Pacific in nineteen thirty-seven," Lisa said. "People in nineteen forty-six, the first year of your New Earth, will recognize her. She had friends, and I think a husband. You'll never get away with it. She's too famous."

"No one will know her as Amelia Earhart," Freemont said, "any more than Lincoln will be recognized. A name can be changed, a face altered. Such things aren't important. The spirit is."

"You'll have to wait years for Amelia to grow up and become a leader."

"Nonsense. Waiting would be an unnecessary delay. I shall fetch her out of the past again—as an adult. The year before she went down in the Pacific will do nicely."

"You can't take two Amelia Earharts with you," Lisa said, temper heating. She repeated, "Leave us behind."

"On this island? Surely you prefer the law-abiding earth of nineteen forty-six. Here you and little Amelia will stay for the rest of your lives."

"We'll get off somehow," Lisa declared.

"On that you are sadly mistaken," Freemont said. "When I leave, I'll reverse the process by which the island was brought into today. I'll send it back a million years to its rightful place in time. What will you find *if* you reach the mainland? Motels, cars, supermarkets? Laundry machines? Toothpaste? Dear me, no! Your raft will carry you where flesh eaters prowl."

Lisa searched Freemont's face for a clue to whether he was serious.

Freemont gave an unhealthy laugh. "Don't look so confused, Lisa. You'll survive. Eat the flesh eaters before they eat you. Perhaps you'll get lucky. Another time traveler may stumble into a wrong corridor and rescue you."

"You can't leave us here!" Lisa said, her voice pitched with emotion. "If you can send the island back a million years, why can't you return Amelia to her backyard?"

"Because I am unsure of memory," Freemont confessed bluntly. "Suppose memories of this island, even if merely dim, shadowy outlines, haunt her? It would be enough to cause a difference in her behavior. The smallest difference will affect the future."

"If I die first, Amelia will be alone!"

"That's not an altogether gloomy fate," Freemont remarked dryly. "Think about it. It's a good deal better than broiling summers in Miami. She may grow lonely, but she'll never be mugged."

Lisa was tempted to comment on Freemont's sense of humor. She said instead, "You don't need Amelia and you don't need me. Put us ashore in the present."

"You know I can't. Amelia was snipped out of the past twenty years too soon. George Washington's raft carried you here against all possibility. You see my problem. You are mistakes, and mistakes must be corrected. You come with me or you stay here."

"There's nothing to fear from us," Lisa said doggedly. "If I ever talk about your New Earth, I'll be put away."

"It is not you who worries me. It is Amelia. She is sure to let a word slip. Someone will hear her and believe her. There always is someone." Freemont shrugged ruefully. "No, it must be," he said. "I'm sorry. I won't be spied upon by space probes before I'm ready. One way or another, you both are done with the earth of today."

"You're not much of a sporting man."

"How's that?"

Lisa drew a long breath, then let it out slowly. "Let's have a contest," she suggested. "If I win, Amelia and I go free. If I lose, we go to the sky with you, or we remain here, whichever you say."

Freemont cocked his head and regarded her with pointed interest. "What sort of contest?"

"I'll arm wrestle Ross Barlow."

"You are a case," Freemont remarked, wagging a finger. "Ross bench-presses four hundred pounds."

"I say I can take him."

"He'll break your arm, girl."

"Then name the contest," Lisa said, fearful her voice had betrayed her eagerness. "Let it be just the two of us. You against me."

Freemont hitched his chair nearer. For a good half minute he mulled the challenge.

"Know this, Lisa," he warned. "It is my nature to win. The petty skills of others bore me. I cannot even remember when I was last forced to make an all-out effort in a contest."

He smiled with boyish pride.

The smile told Lisa she had succeeded. She had thrown a desperation punch and hit Freemont flush on his vanity.

"At our first meeting you said you love the sea," she prodded him.

"Not for delivering someone else's yacht. For off-shore cruising and racing."

"I've done a little racing," Lisa admitted.

Freemont chortled. "You've cleaned up your age-group competition around Miami. I went back and watched you last night."

His fingertips strummed the desktop.

"You might just be the best helmsman on this island, my girl. Or just the second best. Tomorrow we shall find out. It's what I need badly—a few hours off, a morning's entertainment. By George, I like it! We shall race, you and I."

"Where?"

"Once around the island."

"And if I win?"

"If you win," Freemont said with measured deliberateness, "you and little Amelia may leave, on one condition. Neither of you will ever speak of what is happening here."

"And if I lose?"

"You will lose, and eventually you and Amelia may have this lovely island all to yourselves."

Chapter 12

Making Ready

Freemont excused himself. When he returned to the office, he said curtly, "Leave me now. Report to Ross Barlow back at the cottage by six o'clock."

"Where is Amelia?"

"Most likely at her barn. You are free to explore the island, but do not enter any of the buildings. Is that clear? Give me your word on it."

Lisa raised her right hand in a playful pose of oath taking. "You have my word," she said, and went outside.

Her word . . . could she really resist the opportunity to observe the giants of the past? Talk with them? Joke with them? *Touch* them?

It would be so easy: Go into the jungle, double back, slip up to a window, and have a chat with Abraham Lincoln or perhaps Thomas Edison or Benjamin Franklin.

Too easy.

The village seemed asleep. The dirt paths were deserted. Unquestionably, Freemont had left the office to issue instructions to his staff: Stay out of the way. But watch.

He's angling for an excuse to maroon Amelia and me on the island—without his suffering a trace of guilt, Lisa thought.

She knew she would never make it as one of New Earth's leaders. She had little desire to lead and even less to follow. At sixteen, she was already in so many ways her own woman. Of that Freemont surely was aware.

So Freemont *wanted* her to break her word and speak with any of his two hundred. In fact, he was banking on it. The challenge to a sailboat race had been accepted too speedily. He never expected the race to come off. No doubt about that.

If I'm caught snooping around the village—beautiful! Lisa thought. Freemont has his excuse; his conscience is clear. I broke my word; I can't be trusted. Better leave Amelia and me behind!

"Sorry," Lisa whispered at Freemont's office window. "I'm not biting. We go tomorrow."

She set off for the barn at an easy jog. The trail took her past the moist odors of rotting underbrush, past the fallen shadows of newly ancient trees, past beds of yellow wildflowers that might still hold in their thickly tangled stems the air of a million years ago.

Amelia was sitting in the little car. Her face sparkled with welcome, and then tightened.

"Lisa," she said. "You look so serious."

Lisa climbed onto the leather seat with her. The privacy was perfect. Nothing could creep up on them except the wind.

Neither spoke immediately. Lisa thrilled anew with the wonder of sitting next to a half-grown Amelia Earhart.

She was born before polio shots, TV, and males who wore earrings. When her first life ended, a phone call cost a nickel. *Made in Japan* spelled junk. Popular music was for dreaming, not screaming.

"There is something you must know," Lisa began.

Lowering her voice to a gentle tone, she peeled off the layers of time. She watched Amelia closely for the slightest sign of unmanageable fear.

She told her of Freemont's ability to travel into the past and bring back people and objects. She told her how Freemont had gathered two hundred of history's greatest men and women. They were to be his task force in shaping New Earth into a better planet than the original. A seat fit for angels, he had said.

Fascination, not fear, gripped Amelia. Her lower lip drooped in rapt attention. Even her eyes, as she stared at Lisa, seemed to be listening.

"New Earth," Lisa said, "will begin as this earth was in nineteen forty-six. The two hundred leaders are being crash-fed today's knowledge right here, on this island. New Earth will catch up with us, just as backward nations catch up when they are supplied with the latest inventions. It's called leapfrogging. In thirty years New Earth will have outstripped this earth."

She had reached the point of explaining Amelia's two lives. There was no stopping now, no changing her mind, no cushioning the facts.

"The barn and everything in it was brought from the past"—she faltered, and it was a long moment before she could bring herself to finish the sentence—"for you to play with while Freemont decides what to do with you."

Amelia scanned the barn as though seeing it for the first time, getting a feeling more than an understanding.

Tell her! shrilled through Lisa's head.

She tried to sound matter-of-fact.

"Dr. Freemont hasn't told the truth," she said. "You didn't faint in your backyard. You're not here to rest and get well. You were supposed to be one of his two hundred leaders."

"Oh, Lisa, how can I be a leader?"

"That's Freemont's problem. Now try to understand. We're not in the year you played on stilts."

Amelia stiffened, like a bunny frozen alert.

"It's nearly a century later," Lisa said. "You've landed in the future."

Something flickered across Amelia's face. It might have been, finally, a glimmer of fear.

She did not break down. The grit that had carried her to the sky was already in her.

She lifted her head. Her expression asked if this was all some horrible practical joke, while a sudden paleness said she knew, somehow, that Lisa spoke the truth.

"In nineteen thirty-seven you took off from Miami in an attempt to be the first woman to fly around the world," Lisa said.

In the dazzle of the past twenty-four hours, she had neglected to ask Freemont for the details of Earhart's death. She knew the two general theories. The first held that President Franklin D. Roosevelt had used her flight to spy on the Japanese, who were then secretly fortifying islands in the Pacific. The Japanese forced down Earhart and her navigator, Fred Noonan, and later executed them. The second theory held that her plane ran out of fuel and landed on the beach of a small Pacific island. Earhart and Noonan died there of thirst.

Either theory was food for nightmares.

Lisa said only, "You were lost over the Pacific. You were thirty-nine years old and one of the most famous women in the world."

Amelia had grown thoughtful. "Will Dr. Freemont hurt us, Lisa?"

"No, he's not an evil man, thank heaven," Lisa answered earnestly. "He just doesn't want us. He brought you into the present at the wrong age. As for me, I blundered onto the island, something even he had not thought possible."

"What will he do?"

"He isn't sure himself," Lisa said. "We're a problem he doesn't know how to solve. He'd like a good reason to sidestep his conscience and leave us here."

"I'll build a signal fire," Amelia asserted. "I can! A boat will pick us up!"

Lisa explained about the time zone: How no outsider could see or feel or hear the island; and she told Amelia of Freemont's threat to send it, with them on it, to its rightful spot in time—before it was swallowed by the sea long before the first person walked on earth.

"Can he do that?"

"I think so."

A shadow fell on Amelia's brow.

"We'll get away," Lisa assured her. "Tomorrow Dr. Freemont and I are going to have a sailboat race. He's agreed to let us go if I win."

"You'll win!"

"I'm going to do my best."

"What if Dr. Freemont cheats?"

"I expect him to try something," Lisa said. "He thinks he can't afford to lose and let us go free. He's afraid we'll spill the beans about New Earth."

"Who would believe us?"

"Not us, you," Lisa replied. "A ten-year-old Amelia Earhart will turn an awful lot of doubters into believers."

She swung her legs to the ground.

"I'll need your help tomorrow," she said.

"What can I do?"

"Come, I'll show you."

For the next two and a half hours they scouted the shoreline like a golfer and her caddy walking the course before a major tournament. Lisa noted every curve and rise.

"Here," she said. "This is the place."

She had halted on the cliff at the southern tip of the island.

"This is the only really blind corner. I can't sail wide in order to see around it. I'd lose too much time. So here is where it will happen."

Amelia looked at her in puzzlement.

"Whatever it takes for Freemont to win tomorrow will happen here," Lisa explained. "You'll have to stand where you are now and wave to me."

"I have a yellow blouse I can wave," Amelia said. "But why—"

"As we sail toward the cliff tomorrow, watch everywhere," Lisa said. "If something suddenly appears out of sight of my boat, something on the water or on the land that wasn't there an instant before, something big and frightening—wave the yellow blouse. I'll see it. I'll be warned. I'll know there's danger ahead before I round the cliff."

Chapter 13

~~~

Race for Freedom

In the morning Ross Barlow brought Lisa to the beach for the boat race with Preston Freemont.

"Hang in there," the big man said.

The encouragement caught Lisa off guard. She was hesitating over a reply when she saw Freemont.

The time-master was chatting with Amelia between a pair of small sailboats drawn well up on the sand.

Behind him stood about a dozen white-clad members of his staff. Beyond them, like the child of eternity, stretched the deep, enormous ocean.

Lisa sniffed into her lungs the salty dampness with its beckoning call of romantic ports and faraway seas. The familiar scent helped her fight off thoughts of losing.

She must not lose. The sea was her realm. She sailed it as expertly as Freemont combed the past.

She had already won a victory. By refusing to peek in on history's greats, she had forced Freemont to keep his word and race.

She allowed herself a feeling of confidence, but not overconfidence. This was to be no ordinary race.

Her opponent had created energy enough to overcome time. Now he had only to overcome a sixteen-year-old girl in a dinky sailboat.

Freemont spotted her and lifted an arm in greeting. "There you are, Lisa," he called brightly.

With Amelia in tow he came across the beach, using a graceful, easygoing stride, white sneakers squirting sand.

Ross Barlow leaned over and whispered, "Good luck, kid."

"Good luck, yourself," Lisa replied with a toss of her head toward the invisible stars.

The big man nodded soberly and slipped away as Freemont drew near.

"Here's your crew," Freemont announced, and handed over Amelia.

So much for stationing her on the cliff, where she could forewarn of danger. Freemont wasn't letting her out of his sight this morning.

Lisa put an arm around Amelia and drew her close.

"The stakes are unchanged?"

"You and Amelia will be set free if you win," Freemont answered.

His cat green eyes flashed like a grin out of the night.

"Lose," he said, "and it will be as agreed. You and Amelia will stay on the island as it was."

He motioned at the two little boats. "Take your pick," he said smugly.

The smugness was well founded. He had given himself an edge.

In a race between sailboats as small as these two, body weight becomes a prime factor. Lighter is faster, and the slender Freemont was lighter.

Lisa guessed that she and Freemont weighed about the same. Throw in Amelia's weight and throw out fair play and sportsmanship. Their boat became the heavier—and slower—by at least sixty pounds.

The weather, too, favored Freemont. The day was clear and cool. The wind blew from the southeast at about ten knots. The waves were small, without whitecaps.

Lisa would have welcomed a tall-masted sloop, cuffing winds, and bullying waves. Such conditions gave her skill the opportunity to show itself. In mild weather, superiority went unused.

She examined the two boats, circling them slowly.

Each was about twelve feet long. Each had a mainsail, a tiller, a rudder, a single thwart on which to sit, a minimum of rigging, and a paddle.

Lisa stopped behind the first boat.

Her large hands tested the machinery by holding the boom in her right and the sheet in her left. She swept the boom through its full arc, tightening and slackening the sheet. She repeated the action with the other boat, judging, trying to decide.

There was no difference.

Near the stern both bore the name Sailrite, a Miami boatbuilder. That accounted for their looking alike. It didn't account for their having exactly the same scratches.

"I'll take either one," Lisa said. "They're about the same."

"They *are* the same," Freemont declared, plainly enjoying himself. "I beamed her in twice from Miami at dawn. It's only fair I make things absolutely even, don't you agree?"

Lisa bit her tongue to keep from answering.

"See Abe Lincoln on the cliff?" Freemont asked.

Atop the cliff that shouldered the beach were two young men. One was the young Lincoln. The other held a checkered flag.

"The German composer Beethoven," Freemont said. "Lincoln will declare the winner if it's close. Beethoven is the starter. When he whips the flag down, we go."

"Once around the island?"

"Yes, we start and finish where they stand."

Freemont bowed in a courtly fashion and took his leave with a wry, "We shall have a time of it, eh?"

Four of his staff hurried forward. They carried his boat into the shallows.

Freemont hopped in when the water reached his knees. Kneeling in the bow, he paddled directly into the breakers on the way to the calmer water beyond.

Lisa waved off help. She dragged her boat to the water by herself.

"Upsy-daisy," she sang, swinging Amelia aboard. She set her down on the thwart, gingerly settled in beside her, and paddled past the breakers.

Freemont had hoisted sail. He was maneuvering smartly, making a display of his seamanship.

Lisa ignored him and attended to business. She wrestled the rudder and tiller into the fittings and eased the centerboard down into the water. She pulled the halyard hand over hand and watched the single sail unfold and rise upon the mast.

The sail quivered and flapped. The boat swerved, sliding forward and sideways. The hull spoke in its sloshing and gurgling tongue. Bubbles floated behind.

Lisa grabbed the tiller and everything came together—the hull sounds . . . the wavelets building and overturning . . . the boat lifting and falling . . . the forces filling the sail . . . bubbles. The feeling.

"We're under way!" she shouted.

Amelia clapped her hands.

"Dr. Freemont," she said, "told me that you're the best young sailor in Florida!"

"Dunno that," Lisa replied. "I grew up around boats. My dad has been a dockmaster in Miami for thirty years. My mom is a real salt, too. If you love your parents, it's easy to love what they love."

Amelia pushed back a wisp of hair from her eye and frowned. "Why does Dr. Freemont think he must beat you? He can do with us what he wants."

Lisa wished the question had a simple answer.

She said, "Dr. Freemont couldn't be true to the ideals of his New Earth if he did what he wants without giving us a fighting chance."

"But why make it something you're so good at?"

"I guess," Lisa said, "the man has to be the best at everything. Let him meet a great golfer, or a great card player, or a great pencil sharpener and it would be like putting a match to gas. He'd jump to prove he was better."

The conversation had briefly turned Lisa's attention from the other boat. When she glanced across the water again, it was to see Freemont come about, jolting and pitching.

Without having given a preparatory signal, he was racing.

His bow veered across the starting line formed by Lincoln and Beethoven. Beethoven raised the flag above his head and whipped it down.

Freemont had stolen the lead and made it look unplanned.

Lisa refused to be angered or rattled. She worked into position and pursued. In a few minutes, both boats sailed past the cliff. Freemont maintained his lead as they turned south and beat upwind.

"We'll try to stay close till we round the cliff at the other end of the island," Lisa said. "The wind comes off the starboard quarter there, and we'll go a lot faster. We'll overtake him. Don't worry."

In the meantime, she had to use all her skills to keep Freemont's lighter boat within striking range.

Sailing south put the source of the wind on the far side of the island, weakening its force. Nonetheless, it was strong enough to cause a heel, though not strong enough to require hiking out—hanging over the water to balance the boat. Lisa had Amelia slide from side to side with her, according to the tack. Together they held the little boat where it sailed best.

Ahead of them Freemont's craft was heeling, too. He didn't bother to counter the tilt by continually moving his weight, as did Lisa and Amelia.

The error was minor, but revealing.

Preston Freemont was not yet the world's greatest sailor.

Just then the wind softened in his sail. It fluttered and died.

The boat stalled.

Freemont corrected his error promptly. He yanked the sheet and then let it out to near its former setting.

So the great man knew what to do in a minor emergency. On the other hand, the stall pointed up a failing.

It was that his knowledge of racing came from a how-to-sail manual rather than from a blend of inborn talent and experience. What Lisa did so well—respond to the shifting forces and changing angles by feel alone—Freemont could not yet do.

They were approaching the southern end of the island and the cliff where Lisa had thought to station Amelia. Until now, nothing unnatural had occurred.

Freemont began glancing back more often. Despite his weight advantage, he had not left the two girls hopelessly behind.

The boats turned the corner into the windward side of the island. Ahead lay the final leg down the eastern shore. At its end was the finish line, the cliff whereon Abe Lincoln waited to proclaim the winner.

Lisa felt the sheet tugging in her grip and a tickling on the back of her ears. At last she had what she needed desperately—a strong, clean wind off the starboard quarter.

This was it, and never was she so ready for anything in her life. "Here we go, Amelia!"

She kept the sail finely trimmed. She found the line and, by adjusting for any shift in the wind, she coaxed out every bit of speed.

"We're gaining!" Amelia cried.

And all at once she shrieked a warning.

The wild and impossible scene had come out of nowhere, come so suddenly that Lisa thought it was a trick of sunlight.

Except sunlight is silent and still. The square of ocean ahead of them was alive with sounds like the explosions of cannon. Giant dark shapes tore the surface and pounded it into walls of spray as they breached and crashed around Freemont's helplessly tossing little boat.

Chapter 14

Turmoil in the Water

"Whales!" Amelia yelled.

Lisa had seen whales from the Arctic to the West Indies, but seldom so close inshore. And never before had she seen whales appear from nowhere or behave like these.

They seemed weirdly out of tune with nature. Their movements lacked the customary display of spectacular, effortless power. Within a misty square of ocean, they reared and rolled and dived in a kind of mindless frenzy.

Amelia held on to the mast with both arms. Her eyes had opened wide, but there was no fear in them. She seemed to be gaping in sheer amazement that living things could grow to such scale.

The race had to be abandoned, though victory was near. Forcing a passage through the whales was too great a risk. Lisa did not try.

Running close-hauled, she bore due east, toward the wide ocean. The change of direction began a safe route around the whales.

"We'll be just fine," she said in her best professional tone.

Seconds later the boat lurched and hobbyhorsed. One of the gigantic creatures had burst to the surface nearby in a towering swirl of froth. Its mighty back rose fiercely, ramming the air as though breaking through a foot of new ice. A patch of white gleamed under its chin.

The others breached as if seeking to flee the water. One . . . two . . . three . . . four . . . five . . . at least five of them. All with white patches. All bowheads!

There was something unearthly about encountering bowhead whales this far south. Bowheads lived and died in the icy polar seas of the North. They simply didn't exist in tropical zones.

Yet here they were.

Lisa watched them, marveling.

"Look over there!" Amelia shouted.

Freemont's sailboat had been whacked five feet off the water. Freemont flew higher still. He hung helplessly, upside down, back arched, arms and legs widespread.

For an instant man and boat remained like cutout figures tacked to a painted sky. The image shattered as they dropped back among the whales. Steep white splashes soared skyward.

Amelia looked at Lisa pleadingly.

"We'll get him," Lisa promised.

When she glanced again at the spot where Freemont had been, there was nothing. The heaving, changing swells had wiped the surface clean.

Lisa stood up for a better view. Icy cold spray splattered her face.

She hollered Freemont's name with all her power. Only the deafening booms of whales and waves colliding came back to her.

Off to starboard a bowhead smacked the water with its flukes. The impact flushed Freemont, clinging to the keel of his overturned boat, out of a trough. He was shot like a surfboard onto a crest fifty feet from Lisa and Amelia.

Freemont stayed calm. Indeed, he seemed almost scornful of the danger around him. He signaled Lisa to come and get him as haughtily as a New Yorker commands a taxicab to the curb.

Two attempts to come alongside failed. Lisa dropped the sail and seized the paddle.

For a while she made scant headway. Gradually, however, the distance shortened. The two boats bumped.

Freemont grabbed the paddle by the blade end. Lisa and Amelia managed to yank him aboard without overturning.

They made room in the stern. Freemont sank down, shivering.

"Nicely done," he mumbled.

Two words. Lisa knew they weren't easy for

Freemont to get out. They must have twisted his guts and his pride. Having to be grateful was an admission of weakness. "Nicely done" was probably as close as he'd ever come to saying "thank you."

Even to someone for saving his life.

Lisa raised the sail and ran with the wind, using all her skill, all her anticipation.

The little boat pitched and rolled. She survived the flukes of two raging whales—one nearly stood her on her rudder—and reached safe water. There she traveled freely, not laboring anymore.

Lisa was minding the curve of the sail when it came to her.

She trailed her fingers in the warm ocean to make sure.

"I was catching up," she said. "You knew I was going to beat you, didn't you?"

A scornful, ugly hardness spread across Freemont's face.

Lisa flicked drops of water off her fingers.

She said, "Hilda really botched it good this time."

"You're talking rubbish," Freemont snapped.

"You told her to put whales on the far side of the cliff—behind you and in front of me—if I was catching up, right? And I was. But Hilda put them down badly, on top of you. That's missing worse than when she landed Amelia's barn on top of a tree. The idea was for the whales to stop me. Instead they stopped you."

Freemont stared straight ahead and said nothing.

"Hilda should have chosen killer whales," Lisa continued. "I never would have suspected a beaming. Killer whales can live in all the oceans. Bowheads were a goof. They don't swim this far south."

"That's idiot talk," Freemont scoffed.

"Is it? Then why is the water by the whales as cold as the Arctic Ocean? Out farther, it's as nice and warm as Grandma's kitchen. Feel it."

Freemont folded his hands on his lap. "You're imagining."

"I didn't imagine what we both saw. Those bowheads acted crazy. They were terrified. Zip arctic whales to the tropics and see what happens when warm streams from the surrounding water strike them. They'll go crazy trying to escape."

Freemont gestured for Lisa to stop. "Enough," he ordered. "Let it be. I was ahead until the whales. I won't hear more."

"Nothing doing," Lisa said, anger and courage feeding each other. "It's our lives. You gave your word. Honor it. You can't sail an upside-down boat. You couldn't have won."

Again the gesture to stop.

"You didn't beat me, girl," Freemont muttered. "We didn't finish."

"Ask your people who won," Lisa said relentlessly.

Freemont refused to glance at the beach, where members of his staff still stood clotted together, observing. He sat hunched over with his face hidden in the shadows of his arms. He seemed shrunken, old, and dangerous. There was no telling what he might do. Defeat and exhaustion might have worn through his self-control and freed the demon of revenge.

The very real possibility of a charging mammoth in her future darted through Lisa's head.

It was not to happen.

Slowly, slowly Freemont sat up, shoulders squaring as if forcing out his shame and his guilt.

"All right, you won," he admitted wearily. His teeth showed in a half-mocking, half-noble smile of consent. "So be it."

Chapter 15

Childhood II—Again

After Lisa had showered and changed into dry cloth-ing, she joined Amelia in Freemont's office.

The time-master had recovered from his skid into shame. He was, as whenever he chose to be, charming.

"You have appealed to my better nature," he ban-tered. "What do you say to leaving in *Childhood II*?"

"You found her?"

"At the bottom of the ocean. Hitting Washington's raft opened a slit in the bow. She went down off the Caicos Islands. I had my people time-trace her."

"Beam her here," Lisa exclaimed, "before the hole was put in her!"

"Before you were on board," Freemont added good-humoredly. "One sixteen-year-old on her own is quite enough of a headache. Two of you and we'd all go to pieces."

"I had her berthed in Florida at the Miami Marina," Lisa said. "She was fueled and stocked with food and water by nine o'clock on the fifth, the night before I put out for Saint Thomas."

"You slept aboard?"

"No, at home. I got to the boat at six o'clock the next morning. So any time between nine and six is okay. You'll find her in slip eighteen."

Freemont excused himself and left the office for a while. He wore a self-satisfied air upon his return.

"Done," he announced. "How soon can you sail?"

"Now," Lisa answered.

Freemont strolled to the door, his lips parting in lazy amusement. "You can thank me on the way."

Childhood II was tied to a flimsy wooden dock in a cove west of the village.

"I've had clothing for you put in the starboard settee locker," Freemont informed Amelia.

He stooped and kissed her lightly on the forehead. "Have a good life, young lady," he said with genuine tenderness.

"Thank you, sir," she replied respectfully, and started for the boat.

Lisa untied the docking lines.

"You're making it too easy," she accused Freemont.

"Lisa, Lisa," he said, shaking his head. "You must develop the habit of bagging your mistrust. Not all things end with fireworks or treachery. Some things end peacefully and in good faith, like this. We understand each other?"

"The secret of this island is safe with me," Lisa said, "and with Amelia."

"It better be," Freemont replied with a swift, deadly look. "A slip of the tongue, and the truth virus will spread from continent to continent. It carries a disease called global panic."

He paused to observe Amelia climb aboard *Childhood II* and enter the cabin to look around.

"A word of advice," he murmured into Lisa's ear. "She doesn't like to spend time preparing. She wants to be doing right off. That's worth remembering."

"I'll remember."

Freemont made as if to go, changed his mind, and smiled. "I liked you from the beginning."

"I know you did," Lisa replied. "I was counting on it."

"I had rather hoped you'd come along," he said in a voice that was curiously moving.

Lisa wanted to answer with something as warm and flattering. She didn't quite know what.

She settled for a limp, "Good-bye, Doctor, and thank you."

"Good-bye, Lisa." Freemont swept his arm along old planet earth's horizon. "I leave you with the bones of plenty."

They shook hands.

Lisa stepped on deck and into the cockpit. The engine kicked over on the first turn of the key.

She cast a glance toward the dock, thinking to wave a last farewell. It was empty.

Recess was ended, the morning's sport finished. The time-master had returned to the labors of the mind. He had undoubtedly forgotten the sailboat race as quickly as one forgets a robin. Shortly he would forget Lisa Maddock and the young Amelia Earhart.

"Will Dr. Freemont really put another earth in the sky?" Amelia asked.

"I'm sure he will. After that . . ."

"What?"

Lisa buttoned down her misgivings. Freemont had conquered time, but not the unknown caverns of space. The slightest glitch, an error as tiny as a misplaced decimal point, would doom New Earth to wander the universe forever, a traveling creep show of death and decay.

"Freemont will leave our earth alone," Lisa said, partly for Amelia's sake, partly because she wished to believe so. "He honored the agreement. He let us go. He trusts us. We must trust him. We have no choice, do we?"

With that she fell silent. Guiding the sloop out of the tight cove demanded her concentration. Once in the open sea, she turned the bow south by east, toward Saint Thomas.

Amelia suddenly gave a queer kind of gasp. Her attention had fixed on something.

Lisa searched the shore.

A figure in mannish attire had emerged from the jungle and stood motionless on a ledge of rock.

Lisa switched to the automatic pilot and dashed below for binoculars. She knew even as she lifted them to her eyes what she would see.

The figure was a woman in her late thirties. Her bobbed hair set off the boyish beauty of her face. She wore boots and khaki pants. A white scarf was wrapped around her throat and tucked into a knee-length leather flying jacket.

Freemont had done what he said he would.

"Can I see?" Amelia asked.

Lisa passed the binoculars.

Amelia peered through them. "She's very pretty. Will I be as pretty?"

"I'm sure you will."

Amelia lowered the glasses. "Is she the grown-up me?"

"I think so. . . . I mean, yes, she is."

Amelia trembled with pleasure. "I won't have freckles anymore!" she blurted gleefully.

A woman in white stepped onto the ledge. She took the grown Amelia Earhart by the elbow and wrist and led her, as one might lead a sleepwalker, back into the jungle.

The ledge and the jungle stayed there for another

few minutes. Then they weren't. The ocean closed over them. The island vanished in the broad sunlight.

The sight of the bare, flat Atlantic moving where an instant before trees had grown was overwhelming. Amelia gave a single horrified whimper. Lisa, who knew it must happen, nevertheless had to steel herself to keep from crying out.

When she felt her voice wouldn't crack, she reminded Amelia of the island's time zone. They had sailed beyond it.

Two days over the horizon lay Saint Thomas, where tourists charged from the cruise ships to the duty-free shops. Within three weeks Amelia would be in Miami, starting point of her last flight.

Lisa began describing some of the things awaiting her. Television. Space centers. Vitamin pills. Computers. Chinese takeout. She made it fun.

"Will your friends like me?" Amelia asked.

"They'd better, or I'll get new friends. You'll fit in, don't worry. You'll have to do a bit of updating, though. The first step is to choose another name."

"Eunice," she said immediately. "It means 'happy victory' in Greek or Italian. Amelia sounds like a dead flower. I made my sister call me Eunice when we were alone."

"And a last name?"

"Oh, I have one, too—Maddock," she said. "I have to curl my upper lip and growl some to say it. It's a two-fisted name, Daddy would say."

Eunice Maddock. The name throbbed.

Having Amelia take it was like . . . well, finding a kid sister. That close a relationship had never occurred to Lisa before. Now it seemed so obvious and right. Who else was there?

No one else. Letting strangers adopt a ten-year-old from 1908 was madness. Placing her in a foster home was unthinkable.

She belonged in one home only. The freckle-faced girl who had once been world-famous would be the second child the Maddocks had wanted so badly.

Amelia was a gift from the treasury of time. Nevertheless, life with her would not always be smooth and easy.

Take one dockmaster's hardy daughter with a love of boats and the sea. Add a beautiful kid sister whose ambition would sweep all before her. The mix foretold some rocky going.

I'll have to accept playing second fiddle and be proud of her, Lisa thought. Someday I may be known as the governor's big sister. Or the president's.

"You'll come home with me," Lisa said. "Would you like that?"

Amelia's face lit. She uttered a squeal of joy and threw her arms around Lisa's neck.

In the closeness of the embrace it seemed to Lisa as if one heart were pumping blood through both of them.

Amelia stepped back. "What will you tell your mother and father about me?"

"That you're a stowaway," said Lisa, mind racing. "You were born . . . in the Caribbean, but you don't know where. You lived with your parents on their yacht. . . . They died when you were five. A couple who also lived on a yacht took you in. . . . They treated you like a slave. Finally they abandoned you on the pier at Saint Thomas and sailed off. You stowed away aboard the ketch I'm under contract to take back to Miami. How's that?"

"Will your mother and father believe us?"

"Maybe, after I do a little polishing. Maybe not. But they'll love you and want you. In a few months they'll give up tracing roots that have been lost at sea."

Even as she said this, it occurred to her that Amelia was not the only one starting a new life.

Until now she had held independence as her dearest goal. Over the years, while learning to do things on her own, she had lost sight of the truth. Her independence had sprung from an abiding self-interest.

She owed her awakening to Freemont. The time-master had given her Amelia and what Lisa too often had missed in her years. The gift of sharing.

She recalled Amelia's mentioning her love of horses when they had met. She said, "There are riding clubs in the Redlands you can join. And we can go for day sails around Miami or weekend cruises to the Keys. Wherever you go, your secret stays locked inside you, right?"

Amelia nodded gravely. "I must not tell anybody who I really am so long as I live."

She seemed to consider that for a spell.

"When I'm big and know lots of words, I'll write a book about you and me and Dr. Freemont," she said. "I'll make believe it's just a story I made up."

Lisa didn't further the idea by arguing against it. "You'll need a title," she said, and offered, *"Once beyond a Time."*

"That's a swell one," Amelia declared enthusiastically. She seemed content to leave the subject to a forgettable slot in the future.

Lisa was equally content that the work would never see print. It was too lengthy an undertaking. Amelia would always have other, less drawn-out things to do first.

Childhood II chugged on steadily.

Amelia grew restless with just sitting around. She begged to steer. Lisa let her have the wheel, cautioned her to keep the bow on the same compass setting, and slipped below.

She squeezed behind the tiny folding desk and unrolled a chart. Using the island's position, which Freemont had given her on the walk to the dock, she plotted the course for Saint Thomas.

She was stowing the chart when the full force

of her three days on the island overtook her. They were scary and unnatural days, and the luckiest of her life.

For she had met Preston Freemont.

She lacked the wits ever to understand him. But suddenly she no longer misunderstood him.

Granted he had his dark side in the use of threats and power to protect the secret of his New Earth. He was a man who started where other men quit, a man who had to know everything under the sun and above.

He was the dream shaper supreme. Before meeting him, she hadn't known what a human being could be.

She went on deck and halted beside the mast. "Make New Earth a seat fit for angels," she whispered across the water.

Overhead a lone cloud moved in a sapphire sky. A west wind, rare in the region but perfect for the run to Saint Thomas, was freshening. Lisa hoisted the mainsail and jib and cut the engine. *Childhood II* skimmed through the chop as if rejoicing at her rebirth.

In the evening all the stars broke out.

Amelia talked about her life in Kansas and Iowa and the family and friends she would never see again.

And suddenly, in the shelter of the night, the tears came. She laid her cheek on Lisa's lap and sobbed.

"You must leave all the past behind," Lisa said softly, and wished the truth were not so cruel.

The moon had risen by the time Amelia fell asleep. Lisa carried her into the forward bunk, made her comfortable, and tucked a blanket around her. She reduced sail, set the wind-vane steerer, and lay down on the port settee.

Twice during the night she awoke to hear Amelia weeping the fright and sorrow out of her bones. By dawn the sounds of grief were replaced by footsteps padding on deck.

Lisa found her sitting in the bow, bathed in the light of the new day.

"Breakfast in five minutes," she announced. "How do you like your eggs, Amelia?"

The time-child rose and went over and put her hands on her sister's shoulders, her dry eyes shining.

"My name is Eunice," she said.